PREHISTORIC LIFE

INSECTS, BUGS
AND OTHER INVERTEBRATES

BY CLARE HIBBERT AND RUDOLF FARKAS

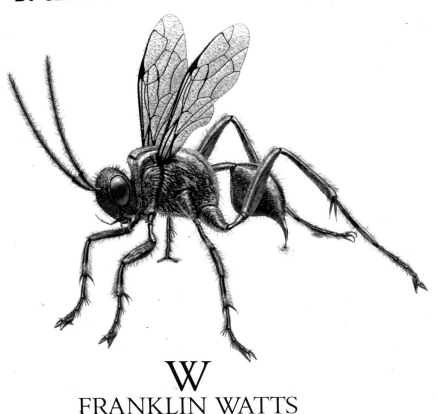

W
FRANKLIN WATTS
LONDON • SYDNEY

Franklin Watts
First published in Great Britain in 2019 by The Watts Publishing Group
Copyright © The Watts Publishing Group 2019

Credits
Series Editor: Amy Pimperton
Series Designer: Peter Scoulding
Picture Researcher: Diana Morris

Picture credits:
Anders L Damgaard/CC Wikimedia Commons: 4.
Laura Dinraths/Shutterstock: 7t.
Tia Monto/CC Wikimedia Commons: 6.
NOAA PD/ Wikimedia Commons: 5.
Nobu Tamura/CC Wikimedia Commons: 7b.

HB ISBN   978 1 4451 5914 0
PB ISBN   978 1 4451 5915 7

Printed in China

Franklin Watts
An imprint of
Hachette Children's Group
Part of The Watts Publishing Group
Carmelite House
50 Victoria Embankment
London EC4Y 0DZ

An Hachette UK Company
www.hachette.co.uk
www.franklinwatts.co.uk

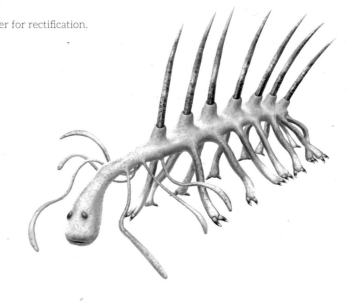

FSC
www.fsc.org
MIX
Paper from
responsible sources
FSC® C104740

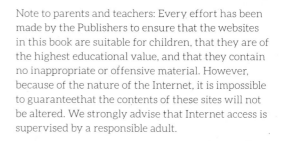

Note to parents and teachers: Every effort has been
made by the Publishers to ensure that the websites
in this book are suitable for children, that they are of
the highest educational value, and that they contain
no inappropriate or offensive material. However,
because of the nature of the Internet, it is impossible
to guaranteethat the contents of these sites will not
be altered. We strongly advise that Internet access is
supervised by a responsible adult.

CONTENTS

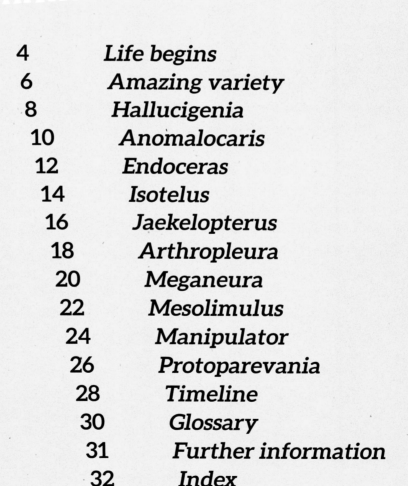

LIFE BEGINS

The Earth took shape from swirling clouds of dust and gas around 4.6 billion years ago (bya).* Within 400 million years, our planet had oceans. These were the birthplace of the first life forms.

Life appears

We know about life long ago because of fossils – the remains of living things that turned into rock over millions of years. However, fossils only show us part of the picture, because many creatures just rot away without leaving a trace. The oldest fossils of living organisms are from around 3.6 bya. They belong to single-celled microbes that appeared at hot spots on the ocean floor.

This ant became trapped inside sticky tree resin, which then fossilised into amber around 40–50 million years ago (mya).

*All the dates in this book are approximate.

Evolving invertebrates

Animals – organisms made up of many cells and able to move, eat and reproduce – evolved about 640 mya. The first ones were sponges, a kind of invertebrate (an animal without a backbone) that still exists today. Other invertebrates include spiders, insects, jellyfish, lobsters and worms. Invertebrates make up 97 per cent of all animal species.

The first life on Earth evolved around hydrothermal vents – holes in the ocean floor where extreme heat leaks from Earth's core.

PREHISTORIC INSECTS

Scientists estimate that the first insects appeared around **480** mya. The oldest known insect fossil was found in Scotland and is about **400** million years old. Insects have three parts to their body and six legs.

Amazing Variety

Over the last billion years, countless invertebrate species have evolved and become extinct. When animals can adapt to big changes in their environment, new species arise. Animals that cannot adapt die out.

Life families

Scientists organise the animal kingdom into major groups called phyla (singular: phylum), which contain creatures that share certain characteristics. About 84 per cent of living animals belong to the phylum known as the arthropods. They include insects, spiders and crabs, as well as extinct groups, such as trilobites, which were extinct by about 252 mya. Molluscs make up the next biggest phylum. They include snails, mussels and squid, as well as the ammonites, which went extinct along with the dinosaurs.

Ammonites were close relatives of octopuses and squid. They had trailing tentacles and a spiral shell and lived in the ocean between 400 and 66 mya.

Crinoids wave their feathery arms to collect food.

SURVIVORS

Crinoids belong to the same phylum as starfish and sea urchins (echinoderms). They appeared around 488 mya, survived several big extinctions and are still around today. They are also known as sea lilies, because they look like flowers.

The crinoid Pentacrinites was common in the Jurassic Period, (201–145 mya).

HALLUCIGENIA

PRONUNCIATION:	Hal-OO-si-JEAN-ee-a
CLASS:	Xenusiids (primitive velvet worms)
LIVED:	Middle Cambrian Period, 520–505 mya
RANGE:	Worldwide
HABITAT:	Oceans
LENGTH:	up to 1.5 cm (0.6 in)

Thumbnail-sized *Hallucigenia* packed many strange features into its small body. Seven pairs of defensive spines stuck out of its back, and it walked along the seabed on seven pairs of squishy legs.

Hallucigenia probably breathed through little holes in its skin. Its long, drooping head had a mouth and a pair of simple eyes, which could tell the difference between light and dark. Teeth around its mouth helped to mash up any food in the water as it was sucked in. There were more needle-like teeth inside *Hallucigenia's* throat that helped to break down food on its journey through the body.

ALL MIXED UP

For many years, palaeontologists didn't have any fossils that showed both *Hallucigenia's* rows of legs, so they pictured it the wrong way up! They thought the spines must be the legs and the legs were waving tentacles. Then, in 1991, palaeontologists found more complete specimens and could see that *Hallucigenia* was very like modern velvet worms.

Like its modern relatives, velvet worms, Hallucigenia had clawed feet for extra grip.

ANOMALOCARIS

PRONUNCIATION:	*a-NOM-alo-CA-ris*
CLASS:	Dinocaridids (primitive arthropods)
LIVED:	Middle Cambrian Period, 508 mya
RANGE:	Worldwide
HABITAT:	Oceans
LENGHT:	1 m (3.3 ft)

Anomalocaris was a large, odd-looking hunter that whooshed through the ocean around 508 mya. Its name, which means 'abnormal shrimp', was chosen because the creature's arms look like shrimps' tails.

SUPER SIGHT

Two fossil eyes found in Australia might have belonged to *Anomalocaris*. They are compound, like a dragonfly's, with more than 16,700 lenses. If those eyes do belong to *Anomalocaris*, the animal had almost 360-degree vision!

Anomalocaris was a primitive ancestor of arthropods, the family of animals that includes crustaceans, spiders and insects. Like them, it had a segmented body and jointed limbs. Its long, spiky arms grasped prey to feed into its circular mouth. Anomalocaris may have hunted hard-shelled trilobites, soft-bodied prey or both. It swam by rippling the flaps along the sides of its body, and waving its fan-shaped tail.

With large, powerful eyes that stuck out on stalks, Anomalocaris probably hunted by sight.

ENDOCERAS

PRONUNCIATION:	EN-do-SE-ruz
CLASS:	Cephalopods
LIVED:	Ordovician Period, 470 mya
RANGE:	Worldwide
HABITAT:	Oceans
WEIGHT:	1,000 kg (2,200 lb)
LENGTH:	3.5 m (11.5 ft)

With a long, pointed shell like a wizard's hat, *Endoceras* lived in warm, shallow seas. It was a cephalopod, like octopuses, squid, cuttlefish and nautiluses. Today, nautiluses are the only cephalopods with shells.

There were many shelled cephalopods 470 million years ago. *Endoceras* was one of the biggest. Its body, or mantle, stayed inside the 3.5-m- (11.5-ft) long protective shell, and its soft, squishy head was at the shell's opening. *Endoceras* used the tentacles that sprouted from its head to grab passing prey and push it into its beak-like mouth. It ambushed other cephalopods, huge sea scorpions and primitive, jawless fish.

BURSTS OF SPEED

Like the modern nautilus, *Endoceras* swam by jet propulsion. It drew water into its mantle (the fleshy part that contained the animal's organs), then pushed the water out through a tube called a siphon. This created a force that propelled *Endoceras* through the water.

Endoceras's shell was made of a reddish-brown mineral called aragonite.

ISOTELUS

PRONUNCIATION:	ISS-o-tell-uz
CLASS:	Trilobites
LIVED:	Ordovician Period, 455 mya
RANGE:	North America
HABITAT:	Oceans
WEIGHT:	7 kg (15.4 lb)
LENGTH:	72 cm (28 in)

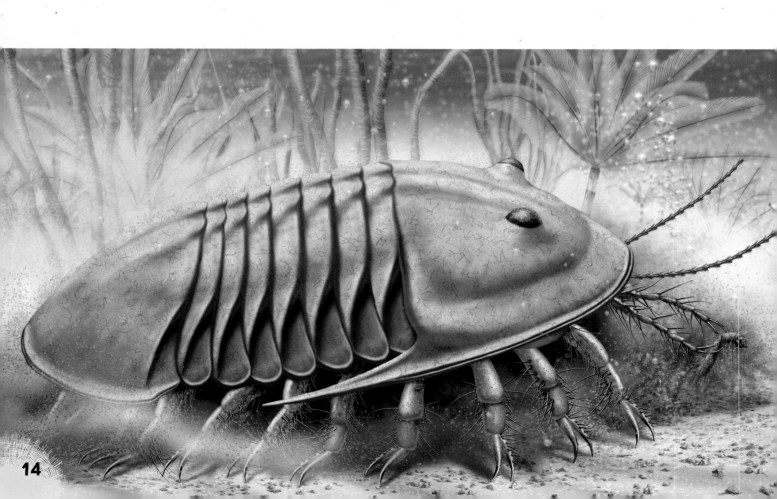

Trilobites were arthropods that looked like giant woodlice. Their closest living relatives today are horseshoe crabs. The largest known trilobite was 72-cm- (28-in) long *Isotelus*, discovered in Manitoba, Canada.

Some trilobites had elaborate spikes or horns for defence or to show off to a mate, but smooth-bodied *Isotelus* simply relied on its size. It was about as big as a skateboard – at least seven times longer than most trilobites. *Isotelus* prowled the sea floor in warm, tropical waters, sometimes scavenging but mostly digging out benthic (burrowing) worms. Its legs had gills for breathing and were also used to grip prey.

EXOSKELETONS

Trilobites were around for nearly 300 million years, and more than 20,000 species are known. Most fossils are not whole creatures but moulted exoskeletons (hard, outer skeletons). Like all arthropods, trilobites shed their exoskeleton as they grew.

Isotelus's shell was made of hard minerals that protected the soft body parts underneath as it hunted prey.

v

JAEKELOPTERUS

PRONUNCIATION:	yay-KLOP-truss
CLASS:	Merostomatas
LIVED:	Devonian Period, 390 mya
RANGE:	Possibly worldwide, but known only from Germany
HABITAT:	Oceans, fresh water
WEIGHT:	387.5 kg (854 lb)
LENGTH:	2.5 m (8.2 ft)

The largest arthropod ever was a sea scorpion called *Jaekelopterus*. Palaeontologists have only found a fossil of one of its claws, but from this they estimate its whole body was as long as a lion's!

Sea scorpions, such as *Jaekelopterus*, weren't really scorpions, but they did have claws and a spiked tail. Some species might have even injected venom, just like scorpions do. Sea scorpions had wide paddles for swimming. They evolved in the sea, but later ones inhabited briny or fresh water. *Jaekelopterus* lived in lakes and rivers. There may have been even larger sea scorpion species that we just haven't found yet.

ROCK STAR

Jaekelopterus's claw was found in a quarry near Prüm, Germany. It had fossilised in what was once the sludge at the bottom of a lake. Over millions of years, the sludge turned into sedimentary rock.

Jaekelopterus used its serrated, pincer-like claws to grasp fish, trilobites, ammonites or smaller sea scorpions, and rip them apart.

ARTHROPLEURA

PRONUNCIATION:	ARTH-ro-PLOO-ra
CLASS:	Millipedes
LIVED:	Carboniferous Period, 315–299 mya
RANGE:	North America and Scotland
HABITAT:	Forests
LENGTH:	2.3 m (7.5 ft)

Coming a close second to *Jaekelopterus* in terms of size, *Arthropleura* is the largest known arthropod to have lived on land. This monstrous millipede was about the same length as a horse.

Arthropleura was a herbivore, not a hunter. It fed on damp and decaying wood, leaves and other plant materials on the forest floor. It was an amazing six times longer than the giant African millipede, which is the largest millipede alive today. Scientists think that arthropods such as *Arthropleura* suddenly grew much larger at this time because of a worldwide increase in oxygen levels.

FEET FIRST

Although the name millipede means 'thousand feet', no known species has that many. *Arthropleura* had **40** pairs of legs. Fossilised *Arthropleura* trackways were uncovered in Nova Scotia, Canada, nearly **150** years ago.

In the face of a predator, such as this huge amphibian Proterogyrinus, Arthropleura *reared up to make itself look bigger.* ∨

MEGANEURA

PRONUNCIATION: meg-ah-NUR-ah
CLASS: Insects
LIVED: Carboniferous Period, 305–299 mya
RANGE: Western Europe and North America
HABITAT: Wetlands
LENGTH: 45 cm (17.7 in)

At least 320 mya, winged insects became the first animals to achieve powered flight, rather than just gliding. One of these early fliers was *Meganeura*, the largest flying insect ever.

AWESOME HUNTER

The adult *Meganeura* hunted primitive reptiles and amphibians as well as other flying insects. Its name means 'big nerved', and describes the lacy veins on its wings. These wings were the size of a wood pigeon's.

Meganeura was a giant griffinfly, closely related to today's dragonflies. Like them, it was a fearsome predator. It spent most of its life as a nymph in water, attacking fish, tadpoles and aquatic insects with its powerful, grasping jaws. Towards the end of its life cycle, *Meganeura* climbed out of the water. Its skin split and its winged, adult body emerged.

Meganeura's record-breaking wings were up to 75 cm (29.5 in) across.

MESOLIMULUS

PRONUNCIATION:	mess-uh-LIM-yoo-luss
CLASS:	Merostomatas
LIVED:	Late Jurassic Period, 151–145 mya
RANGE:	Europe and Asia
HABITAT:	Oceans
LENGTH:	46 cm (18 in)

Horseshoe crabs first appeared 445 mya, and have barely changed in 300 million years. *Mesolimulus*, which swam in Late Jurassic seas, was almost identical to today's Atlantic horseshoe crab.

Like all horseshoe crabs, *Mesolimulus* was a closer relative to spiders than crabs. It fed on molluscs, worms and other invertebrates, hunting by sight. It had nine eyes – two compound ones on each side of its head, five simple eyes on its shell and two more near its mouth. It did not have jaws. It used grains of sand in its gizzard (part of its stomach) to mash up its food so it was digestible.

LOTS OF LEGS

Mesolimulus had six pairs of legs sticking out of its head - one pair for grabbing food and the rest for walking or swimming. Another six pairs stuck out of *Mesolimulus*'s body. Most of these had gills and helped it to breathe underwater.

Mesolimulus's tail, called the telson, acted as a rudder to steer it when swimming.

MANIPULATOR

PRONUNCIATION: man-ip-EW-layt-uh

CLASS: Insects

LIVED: Early Cretaceous Period, 100 mya

RANGE: Myanmar

HABITAT: Forests

LENGTH: 4.5 mm (0.2 in)

From fallen fruit and dead insects to slices of bread, modern cockroaches eat whatever they can find – but they are not usually active predators. The Cretaceous cockroach, *Manipulator*, was different.

Less than half a centimetre long, *Manipulator* was a small but speedy night hunter with long legs for chasing down prey. Its triangular head, supported on a long neck, had large, forward-facing eyes and could turn to point the insect's antennae in different directions. *Manipulator* relied on its eyes and feelers to locate prey on the forest floor. The antennae could smell, taste and touch, and probably also sensed changes in temperature and humidity.

GREEDY GRABBERS

Manipulator's front legs had short, strong spines that helped it to grasp prey – much like a praying mantis's legs. Mantises did evolve from predatory cockroaches, but they are not direct descendants of *Manipulator*.

Manipulator *had a pair of smaller, simpler eyes on the top of its head. These helped detect insect-eating dinosaurs and other predators.*

PROTOPAREVANIA

PRONUNCIATION: pro-toe-pah-rah-VAY-nee-uh
CLASS: Insects
LIVED: Late Cretaceous Period, 80 mya
RANGE: Lebanon, Western Asia
HABITAT: Tropical forests
LENGTH: 1.4 mm (0.06 in)

Protoparevania was a small wasp that had a neat trick – it laid its eggs inside cockroaches' egg cases so that its young had a ready supply of food.

Protoparevania belonged to the ensign wasp family that evolved nearly 150 mya and still exists today. Every species of ensign wasp that scientists have studied is a parasite on cockroaches. The female *Protoparevania* would pierce the tough skin of a cockroach egg case and lay an egg inside. When the larva hatched, it fattened up on cockroach eggs. Then, still inside the protective case, it pupated. The adult wasp used its powerful jaws to chew its way out of the egg case – and the life cycle began again.

SWEET NECTAR

Flowering plants first appeared in the Cretaceous Period, but most of the trees in *Protoparevania's* forest home were non-flowering conifers, cycads and ginkgoes. The adult wasps took to the wing to find flowers and feed on their sugary nectar.

Protoparevania used its antennae, which were as long as its body, to examine an egg case before laying an egg inside.

TIMELINE

This timeline shows the different periods, or chunks of time, since life began on Earth. It includes the appearance of key species in this book, as well as when some of them became extinct.*

Eon

Precambrian 4,600–541 mya

3,600 mya	First life forms – bacteria
640 mya	First animals (sponges) appear

Era   Period

PALAEOZOIC 541–252 mya

Cambrian 541–485 mya

520–505 mya	*Hallucigenia*
508 mya	*Anomalocaris*
488 mya	Crinoids (sea lilies)

Ordovician 485–443 mya

470 mya	*Endoceras*
455 mya	*Isotelus*
455–430 mya	First major extinction wipes out 85 per cent of all species

Silurian 443–419 mya

439 mya	The first plants appear

Devonian 419–359 mya

400 mya	Ammonites, flying insects and first land vertebrates appear
407–359 mya	Second major extinction wipes out 75 per cent of animal species
390 mya	*Jaekelopterus*

(Cont.)

* All the dates on these pages are approximate.

Era	Period		
(Cont.)	**Carboniferous 359–299 mya**		
	315–299 mya	*Arthropleura*	
	305–299 mya	*Meganeura*	

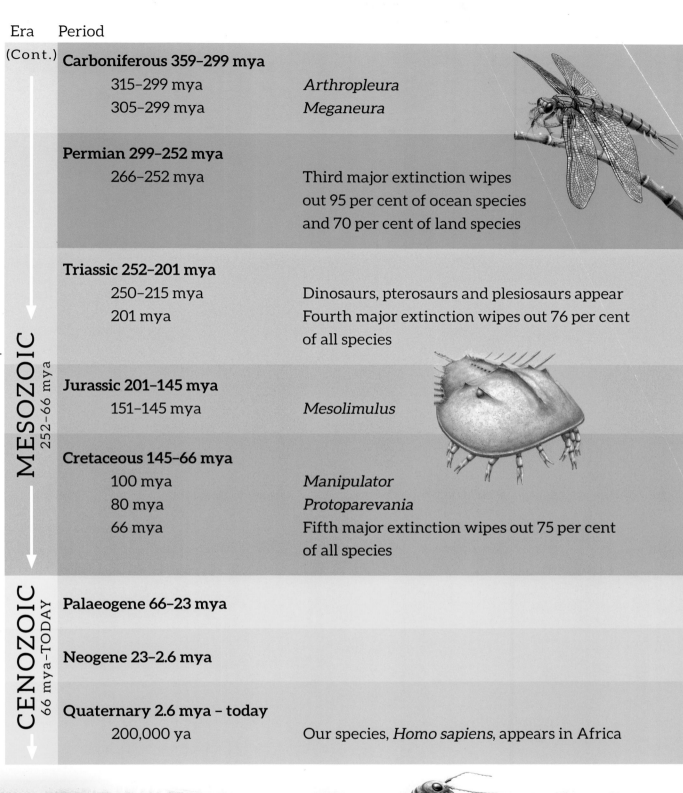

MESOZOIC 252–66 mya

Permian 299–252 mya

266–252 mya — Third major extinction wipes out 95 per cent of ocean species and 70 per cent of land species

Triassic 252–201 mya

250–215 mya — Dinosaurs, pterosaurs and plesiosaurs appear

201 mya — Fourth major extinction wipes out 76 per cent of all species

Jurassic 201–145 mya

151–145 mya — *Mesolimulus*

Cretaceous 145–66 mya

100 mya — *Manipulator*

80 mya — *Protoparevania*

66 mya — Fifth major extinction wipes out 75 per cent of all species

CENOZOIC 66 mya–TODAY

Palaeogene 66–23 mya

Neogene 23–2.6 mya

Quaternary 2.6 mya – today

200,000 ya — Our species, *Homo sapiens*, appears in Africa

GLOSSARY

amphibian An animal with a bony skeleton and slimy skin that lives partly on land, partly in water, and cannot make its own body heat

arthropod An invertebrate with a segmented body, jointed limbs and, usually, an exoskelton or shell

briny salty

cell A tiny, living unit from which all organisms are made

cephalopod A mollusc that has a ring of tentacles around its head

compound eye An eye that is made up of many lenses

dinosaur An extinct land reptile from the Triassic, Jurassic or Cretaceous periods, whose legs came straight down from its body rather than splaying out like a modern reptile's

evolve To change from one species to another over millions of years, by passing on useful characteristics from one generation to the next

extinct Describes an animal or plant that has died out for ever

fossil The remains of an animal or plant that died long ago, preserved in rock

gill One of a pair of frilly organs that are used by fish and other aquatic animals to breathe underwater

gizzard A part of the stomach, with thick, muscular walls that help to grind up food

herbivore A plant-eater

invertebrate An animal without a backbone (insects, spiders, worms, crabs and jellyfish are all invertebrates)

kingdom One of the top scientific groupings of living things. Many scientists split living things into five kingdoms: animals, plants, fungi, protists (protozoa and algae) and monera (bacteria and blue-green algae).

mollusc An invertebrate with a soft, unsegmented body and, usually, a shell

nautilus A cephalopod that has a round, spiral shell

nymph A young insect that is similar to its parent, but will change to reach its adult form

organism Any single living thing, from a microbe to a human being

palaeontologist A scientist who studies fossils

phylum (plural: phyla) A major group of living things within a kingdom (arthropods and molluscs are both phyla in the animal kingdom)

predator An animal that hunts other animals for food

prehistoric From the time before written records

prey An animal that is hunted by other animals for food

pupate The stage when an insect larva becomes an adult

reproduce To make babies, eggs or seeds. Adult animals and plants can reproduce.

reptile An animal with a bony skeleton and scaly skin that cannot make its own body heat

sedimentary rock Rock formed when sand, mud, minerals or plant and animal remains are pressed together until they harden

species One particular type of living thing. Members of the same species look like each other and can reproduce together.

vertebrate An animal with a backbone (fish, amphibians, reptiles and mammals – including humans – are all vertebrates)

FURTHER INFORMATION

Books:

Early Life on Earth by Michael Bright (Wayland, 2016)
Eyewitness: Fossil (DK, 2017)
DK Handbooks: Fossils by Cyril Walker and David Ward (DK, 2010)
Paleo Bugs – Survival of the Creepiest by Timothy J Bradley (Chronicle Books, 2008)
Prehistoric (DK, 2009)
Rock Explorer: Fossils by Claudia Martin (QED Publishing, 2018)
Story of Life: Evolution by Katie Scott (Big Picture Press, 2015)
The Illustrated Handbook of Fossils by Steve Parker (Lorenz Books, 2014)

Websites:

www.bgs.ac.uk/discoveringGeology/time/fossilfocus/
Pages on the British Geological Survey's website dedicated to fossil finds, including many fossilised invertebrates.
www.nationalgeographic.com/animals/prehistoric
National Geographic Magazine's guide to prehistoric creatures
www.prehistoric-wildlife.com
An A-Z guide to prehistoric creatures
ukfossils.co.uk
Advice on fossil hunting in the UK, including good places to look for them and guides on identifying fossil finds.

Places:

The Dinosaur Museum, Dorset
National Museum, Cardiff
National Museum of Scotland, Edinburgh
Natural History Museum, London
Pitt-Rivers Museum, Oxford
Shropshire Hills Discovery Centre, Craven Arms
Ulster Museum, Belfast

INDEX